For Ralph

First U.S. edition 2004

Library of Congress Catalog Card Number 2003116477

ISBN 0-7636-2517-5

10 9 8 7 6 5 4 3 2

Printed in China

This book was typeset in Barmeno.
The illustrations were done in watercolor and cut paper.

Candlewick Press
2067 Massachusetts Avenue
Cambridge, Massachusetts 02140

visit us at www.candlewick.com

CANDLEWICK PRESS
CAMBRIDGE, MASSACHUSETTS

A New House for Mouse

Petr Horáček

One day a little mouse looked out of the
tiny hole where she lived and saw a big apple.

"I would like that apple to eat," said Little Mouse.
"I must bring it inside."

She tried and tried, but she couldn't
pull the apple through the tiny hole.
"My little house is too small," said Little Mouse.
"I'll look for a bigger one."

So off she set.

"Looking for a new house
makes you hungry," said Little Mouse
as she took a few bites of the juicy apple. Then she
spotted a hole that was just a little bigger than hers.
"This looks just right," she said as she looked inside.

"Hello, Mole!
I need a bigger house
for my apple and me.
May I live here with you?"

"I'm sorry," mumbled Mole,
"but my home is too full
of books. I don't think there
is room for both of us."

"I'll keep looking," said Little Mouse.

Soon Little Mouse felt hungry again.

"I'll just have a nibble," she said to herself.

Then she spotted a hole that was just a little bigger

than Mole's. "That will be perfect," she said.

She looked inside.

"Hello, Rabbit," she said.
"I'm looking for a bigger
house for my apple and me.
May I live here with you?"

"I'm sorry," twittered Rabbit,
"but my home is too full of cabbage.
I don't think there is room for
both of us."

"Perhaps not," said Little Mouse.

Little Mouse set off again,
but she was still hungry, so she nibbled
on the apple as she went. Then she spotted another
hole that was just a little bigger than Rabbit's.

"That will be just right," she said. She looked inside.

"Hello, Badger,"
she said. "I am looking
for a new home for my
apple and me. May we
come and live with you?"

"I'm sorry," barked Badger,
"but I stretch out on my cushions
all day, sleeping. I don't think
there's room for both of us."

"Perhaps not," said Little Mouse,
feeling rather tired and still
hungry. She nibbled on the apple
once again.

That evening she came across an enormous hole. "This must be big enough for my apple and me," she thought.

"Hello! Is anybody there?" she shouted.

"Hello, little mouse," growled Bear. "Why don't you come and live here with me?"

"No, thank you," squeaked Little Mouse. "I think the cave is too small for you and me AND my apple."

And off she ran.

Little Mouse was very tired now,
but pulling the apple seemed easier.
Suddenly she saw a tiny hole.
"That looks perfect," she squeaked.
She looked inside.

There was no one at home.
Little Mouse went right in and
pulled her apple behind her.
It fit perfectly.

"I knew I would find somewhere just right
for both me and my apple," she said,
and she climbed into her own bed
and fell fast asleep.

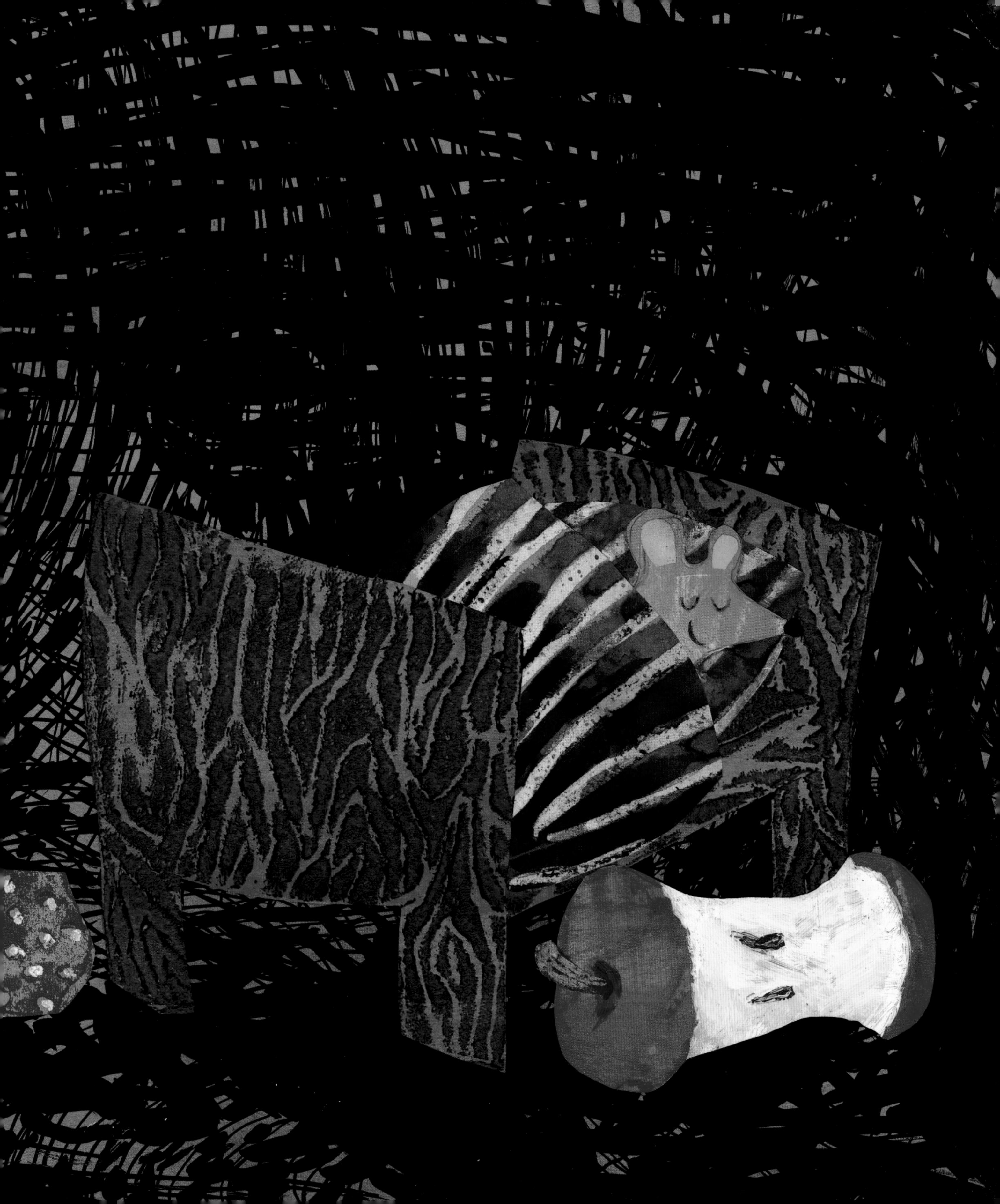